Five-Minute Cozy Mini Mysteries (with Solutions)

26 Whodunits That Test Your Amateur Sleuthing Smarts

LORETTA MARTIN

Cover design: Paul Faber

ISBN: 9798679884748
Imprint: Independently published

Visit author website: http://www.wordygirly.com
This is a work of fiction. Unless otherwise indicated, all
names, characters, businesses, places, events and incidents
in this book are either the product of the author's
imagination or used in a fictitious manner. Any resemblance
to actual persons, living or dead, or actual events, is
purely coincidental.

Dedication

With love and gratitude to Phil and Paul, my two best men, for more reasons than I have words to express. How you've managed to put up with me remains a mystery.

Introduction

Maybe you're familiar with the cozy mystery (*cosy* if you're in the UK). The term was coined in the late 20th Century to describe what's also known as a mini cozy mystery. Since then, this fiction writing sub-genre has blossomed into a substantial, and profitable, niche market.

According to K-lytics, a resource that analyzes e-book marketing trends, between 2012 and 2018, Google bestseller sales ranking for the cozy mystery category improved by up to 55%, while 2018 e-book royalties grew 29% over 2017. In 2019, Book Ad Report announced that crime and mystery fiction overall banked $728.2 million in sales.

What elements comprise a cozy mystery?

The list varies, but most cozies share these basic characteristics:

Plot: This is the "what happens" component, the action. Cozy plots include the usual misdeeds like murder, theft, fraud, and vandalism. They go further by including noncriminal action. In "Secret Bunny," an anonymous admirer finds a "sweet" route to its object of affection. Plot can introduce a teachable moment. In "Halloween Heist," the culprit learns a lesson in a frightful way.

Graphic violence and offensive language: You won't find either in cozies. In "Deadly Misstep," somebody whacked Old Man Wingate over the head, but blood-and-gore details are left out. Nor will you find four-letter bombs or hot sex (although there might be references to infidelity).

Characters: The cast is limited. There's a protagonist (usually female) who cracks the case, with or without a quirky partner. Obviously, there's a victim (or victims), or recipient of a good deed. In these 26 stories, two or three suspects, at most, round out the roles. Protagonists generally are everyday people or small-town officials relying on commonsense logic instead of big-city forensics found in police procedurals. In "Mother's Day Charm," a crossword enthusiast cracks the case. Perps aren't inherently evil but might be driven by greed ("Salon Con") or desperation ("Music Box Blunder").

Setting: Generally, action occurs within a tight time frame and fixed location. In "Ring of Deception" and "Poetic Device," everything happens within 24 hours and in a kitchen. Idealized settings, where bad things rarely happen and everybody knows everybody else, are pillars of the cozy mystery genre.

Finally, there's no pass-or-fail pressure with these 26 mysteries. The only crime you're committing is having fun trying to solve them.

Contents

Deadly Misstep

(A version of this story appeared in *Woman's World*.)

Sheriff Maddy Doyle had just hung up the phone when her deputy, Homer Kramden, arrived with their morning coffee.

"Old Man Wingate's dead," she said.

The call came from Clara Fremont, Wingate's widowed housekeeper of 15 years who lived in the coach house.

Twenty minutes later, they arrived at the Wingate estate, parked the cruiser, and found the medical examiner, Dawson Hodges, at the foot of the spiral stairway, kneeling over the corpse lying face down on the marble floor. A gaping wound was at the base of his skull. Hodges's team was just finishing up before removing the body. "Looks like he tripped," he said, nodding at the robe sash tangled around Wingate's legs. "We'll know more after I get him on the table."

Doyle and Kramden headed to the parlor. Mrs. Fremont and Wingate's niece, Emily Larson, sat across from each

1

other, their faces grim. The sheriff led the housekeeper into the entry hall, while her deputy remained with Miss Larson.

"What happened?" she asked.

"After Mr. Wingate and Miss Emily retired upstairs after dinner, I cleaned up and left around 8:00 and was in bed by 9:30. I arrived this morning at 7:00 to find him l-l-like that," she stammered, close to tears.

"Did you check for a pulse?"

"No, it was obvious he wasn't breathing."

She looked as if she wanted to say more, but didn't, so Doyle changed tracks.

"You live alone?"

"I did until my son, Bobby, moved in with me recently. He stayed in town last night with a friend and hasn't returned yet."

"Please send Miss Larson out and wait in the parlor in case you think of something else."

Doyle watched Emily approach, still in her robe, gripping a balled-up handkerchief. She lived with her bachelor uncle, who adopted her after her parents died in a house fire almost 20 years ago. Now in her 30's and unmarried, she was the town librarian.

"Where were you between 7PM and this morning?" Doyle inquired.

"After dinner, I went to my room, read, and fell asleep sometime after 8:30. At midnight I heard noises downstairs. Thinking it was Uncle, I went to my door and called out, but there was no answer. Assuming he'd gone to his room, I read again until I fell asleep. I woke to Mrs. Fremont's screams and rushed downstairs.

"Did you touch him?"

"*I couldn't!* I can still see that look on his face," she said, shuddering.

"Anything else"?

"Well," Emily hesitated, "last week, I overheard Uncle tell Mrs. Fremont he didn't appreciate Bobby moving in without permission after losing his job. He said he had a bad feeling about him. Just yesterday, he confided to me that he intended to order them both to leave."

As Doyle was adding to her notes, Deputy Kramden returned from the parlor.

"Guess we'll talk to the son next," he said.

"Nope. I think we're done here. You'd better get dressed and come with us, Miss Larson," she said, snapping her notebook shut.

Ω

What tipped the sheriff off?

Solution: Deadly Misstep

Emily couldn't have seen "that look on his face" because he landed face down. After the housekeeper left for the night, she and Wingate were at the top of the stairs when he announced his intention to marry Mrs. Fremont. Enraged and fearing loss of her inheritance, Emily pushed him down the stairs and arranged his sash to make it look like he tripped on it. She fabricated an argument between Wingate and the housekeeper to implicate her and Bobby.

Lucky Lucy

At 7:30AM, the seven-year-old Brennan triplets—Avery, Linus, and Paul—had been locked in stony silence for more than an hour. They'd been confined to the heated ice shanty their dad, Hiram, had rented for ice fishing. They stared glumly out the zippered window at him sitting on his bucket, surrounded by his gear and waiting for the fish. He'd drilled a hole through the ice, baited hooks, and set flags that signaled a bite.

The family had driven 200 miles to attend an annual winter fest, a weekend of snow-plow races, cross-country skiing, snowball-tossing contests, and of course ice fishing. Last night at dinner, Hiram had surprised the boys by presenting each with his own tackle box and pole.

"Tomorrow," he announced, "is men's day on the ice."

"I'll stick to boutiques, ice sculpture and craft exhibits," their mom, Bridget, said over noisy high fives.

The boys enjoyed what they called "Dad's funny fish talk"—ice jiggers, floats, gaff hooks, and lures. He was especially proud of "Lucky Lucy," his three-hook, stainless steel lure.

"Lucy snared my biggest catch ever, a 22-pound largemouth bass," he gloated.

Hiram showed them his tackle box but never allowed them to handle the contents without supervision.

"Gotta watch out for knives, hooks, and lures," he cautioned, pointing to the razor-sharp implements.

Today, what should've been a bonding event had ended up with the boys grounded because one of them had "borrowed" Lucky Lucy.

"Stay right here until somebody's ready to confess," Hiram ordered.

By noon, matters got worse when their mom arrived after her husband phoned to report what happened.

"Alright, who took it?" she demanded, removing her outer wear at once.

"Not me!" Avery protested, waving his gloved hands.

"I didn't take it," Linus insisted, both hands wrapped around a thermos of hot chocolate.

"Me neither," Paul cried, briefly suspending his nervous nail-biting habit.

Bridget stared at each of them.

"You two," she said, pointing, "get out there with Dad."

"You, Mister, let's talk."

Ω
Who took the lure, and what tipped Mom off?

Solution: Lucky Lucy

Seeing that Avery was the only one wearing gloves in the heated shanty, Bridget became suspicious. He wanted to land the first catch, even if it meant being punished. While hastily stuffing it into one of his thick gloves as he helped load gear, he pricked his skin and drew blood. Avery kept his gloves on to hide the wound. He also learned a painful lesson on sportsmanship.

Loretta Martin

Gem Mayhem

"Hurry up, Joyce. The snowplows haven't made it through yet," Brendan Warren said, peering out their bedroom window."

They were due at Grand Pines Lodge in an hour for his parents' 45th anniversary celebration. His sister, Sondra, and her fiancé, Robert, would be joining them. It was only 3PM, but they'd decided on an early dinner because of the heavy snowfall, which hadn't let up.

"It's not here!" Joyce exclaimed, rummaging through her jewelry chest.

"What?"

"Ugly Onyx."

Ugly Onyx was their secret name for the earrings and brooch Brendan's mom, Eloise, gave her last year as a birthday present.

"They're vintage estate gems, a 10th anniversary gift from Herb," Eloise had bragged of the gaudy, clunky clip-ons made of black onyx with white rhinestone accents.

"They feel like lead weights, and that matching banana-shaped brooch is even tackier," Joyce complained to her husband.

9

"Promise you'll wear them on special occasions," Eloise had pressed.

Why me and not Sondra? she wanted to ask. But a promise is a promise she reminded herself.

"Didn't you wear them to Sondra's engagement party?" Brendan asked.

"That was three months ago. I didn't realize they were missing until now."

Just then, their 5-year-old twins, Tessa and Teresa, ran in, followed by Mia Vincent, their 16-year-old babysitter from two doors down.

"They wanted to say goodbye," Mia said.

"Mommy, Aunt Sondra didn't help us with Mr. Frosty today," Tessa fretted.

"That's 'cause she was crying," Teresa said.

"Crying?" Brendan shot Joyce a look.

"The kids and I were building a snowman this morning when Sondra arrived, upset over an argument with Robert. I got the girls settled in their room so we could talk," Joyce explained, keeping her tone light for the girls' sake.

"Off you go, ladies. If you're good, Mia might let you watch TV for an hour before bed," Brendan said after hugs all around.

"Is Sondra okay?" he asked, turning to Joyce after everyone had left the room.

"It was something silly, pre-wedding jitters. We talked over tea while she calmed down. She went upstairs to wash her face before leaving, humming the wedding march."

"Another argument for elopement. Now find Ugly Onyx so we can get going."

"It was in a pouch inside this chest. How can I explain this to Eloise?" she said on their way to the garage.

"Tell her aliens took it but left the good stuff behind."

"That's not funny. Watch out for the snowman, she said, checking her makeup in the mirror."

"I'll shovel first thing tomorrow," Brendan said, carefully maneuvering down the driveway.

"I hate to spoil her evening," Joyce said.

"Don't worry, you won't," he said, laughing as he shifted into reverse.

"Why're we backing up, and what's so funny?"

Ω

Why was Brendan laughing?

Solution: Gem Mayhem

The twins "borrowed" Ugly Onyx during Sondra's visit. They sneaked out while their parents were getting ready and before the sitter arrived. They gave Mr. Frosty a carrot nose, eyes using the earrings, and a smiling mouth using the banana-shaped brooch. Brendan spotted the glittering features while navigating the driveway.

Murder or Suicide?

At 10AM, Nora Foster, a reporter, heard the dispatcher on her TV newsroom scanner: "55 Suncrest Drive, possible self-inflicted gunshot wound. Unresponsive female. EMS unit 665 and cruiser 24 en route."

Minutes later, she arrived at the scene and raced up the stairs where first responders waited outside a bedroom.

"Hold it there, Foster, you know better than to contaminate my scene," Sheriff Sam Dunham said with his usual gruffness.

From where she stood, Nora saw Bethany Linden, a 44-year-old socialite, slumped in a wingback chair, a fatal gunshot wound on her right temple. A small caliber pistol dangled from her right hand.

"At least tell me who called it in, Sam."

"The nephew," he motioned to a young man just inside the doorway. "Now let me do my job."

Pete Sauer, 25, was quite handsome, except for chalk-white skin that contrasted sharply to the scarlet beach cover-up and black swim trunks he wore. Nora noticed his earthy cologne at once, the same sandalwood scent her boyfriend liked. She took notes while he gave his statement.

"My aunt hired me as her personal assistant so I could save enough to spend a year in Europe after grad school. She let me stay in the apartment over the garage, rent free, and gave me full access to the swimming pool. Because she hadn't hired another housekeeper yet since firing Mrs. Ivers, I also fixed meals and did housework."

"Why'd she fire the housekeeper?"

"Aunt Bethany accused her of stealing."

"What else?" the sheriff asked, making a note to interview Mrs. Ivers.

"We had a routine. I was up by 7:00, swam for an hour, and let myself in to start coffee. Then I went back to my apartment to shower and dress. I had breakfast ready by 9:00. My aunt spent breakfast making a list of my chores for the day."

"You had meals together?"

"She didn't like eating alone and was depressed over her husband leaving her for a younger woman. Her drinking had gotten out of control as well. I should've seen this coming."

"You followed the same routine this morning?"

"Hardly. I was making coffee when I heard the gunshot coming from upstairs."

"Then what?"

"I ran back up, found her . . . like that and dialed 911."

"Wait downstairs while I look around some more."

When Mark left, the sheriff saw Nora still writing.

"You still hanging around, Foster?"

"It's a good thing I am. You'll thank me later."

Ω

What did Nora Foster know?

Solution: Murder or Suicide?

As Nora explained to Sheriff Dunham, swimming in chlorinated water causes chlorine to bind to skin and hair, leaving a distinct odor. She smelled Pete's cologne but no hint of chlorine because he never took a shower. He incriminated himself by inadvertently saying he ran *back* upstairs. Bethany had refused to finance his European junket, insisting he work for it, including performing housework, a further blow to his ego. Pete knew where she kept a gun and shot her and staged a suicide.

Ring of Deception

A ndy, I've looked *everywhere!*" Aunt Lynn cried. He pictured her working the cord on her landline phone like a string of worry beads.

The diamond ring that Uncle Bert gave her almost 50 years ago was missing.

"I'm sure I left it on the kitchen counter yesterday, but, well . . . maybe—"

"—We'll find it, don't worry. Promise you'll wait for me before calling the police, okay?"

"Hmm? Alright."

Distracted, Lynn Ogden hung up. At 80, she'd become more absent-minded since her husband died last year. This wouldn't be the first time something had "gone missing." A few days ago, Andy caught his favorite aunt putting the oatmeal box in the freezer.

He smiled, remembering how, as a boy, he helped his favorite aunt bake cookies on days he didn't have school. He'd peer through the oven door every few minutes, willing them to bake faster, making her laugh.

Daylight savings time had ended two days ago, so it was almost dark when he arrived at the rambling Victorian at

16

4:30. Apparently, his aunt had forgotten her promise, because Sheriff Jill Lester's cruiser was in the driveway. The rusty pickup belonging to Hugo and Anya Lundgren was parked farther down the drive, near a shed. After Uncle Bert died, Andy hired the Lundgrens to help keep the place running because his aunt refused to move.

"I spent the best years of my life in this house, and I'll spend my last ones here as well," she protested.

On the way to the back door, which everyone used, Andy almost tripped on a step, a reminder to have Hugo replace the porch lightbulb. Aunt Lynn and Sheriff Lester were seated at the kitchen table. Hugo stood nearby, and Anya was pouring ice tea into glasses. The clink of ice cubes echoed in the huge kitchen. After serving everyone, Anya poured tea in her thermos.

"Your aunt was just giving me her statement. Go on, Mrs. Ogden."

"I returned from the shed, where Hugo was sanding shutters. It was almost 2:30. I remember because that's when my favorite soap opera starts. I took my ring off to rinse the sawdust off and laid it on the counter. Then, Milly from next door knocked—we watch the show together while having tea in the parlor. She left a half hour later."

"Anya, where were you?"

"Upstairs, ma'am. Cleaning."

"What did you do after Milly left, Mrs. Ogden?"

"Well, I started upstairs but noticed the kitchen wall clock hadn't been reset, so I called Anya down to change it. Then I continued up to my sewing room."

"When did you and Hugo leave?" she asked the housekeeper.

"Around 5:30."

"And returned when?"

"6AM."

"Did you see the ring on the counter?"

"No ma'am."

"What exactly did you do upon arriving?"

"Let myself in, checked the counter for any instructions Mrs. Ogden might've written, turned on lights, and refilled ice trays. She forgets, so I store cubes in freezer bags."

"And you, Hugo?"

"I let Anya out at the back porch, parked, and then started my chores."

"How'd you hurt yourself?" she asked, nodding at his bandaged hand.

"I forgot my flashlight and stumbled in the dark while getting out of my truck."

"Who else has keys, Mrs. Ogden?"

"Just the Lundgrens and Andy.

"Let's go over this again," Sheriff Lester said, staring daggers at one of them.

Ω

Which story raised Sheriff Lester's suspicions?

Solution: Ring of Deception

Anya stole the ring during Milly's visit. It was still dark at 6:00 (Hugo stumbled). The porch light was out (Andy tripped). How could Anya "see" there was no ring on the counter *before* turning on lights? Everyone else was drinking ice tea from glasses, but Anya used her thermos, which contained the ice cube in which she'd stashed the ring earlier.

One of a Kind

Brenda Collins, a member of the ladies auxiliary, burst into the church's downstairs office, where Felice Parker was reviewing this year's Memorial Day activities. The parade had been scheduled for Monday the 25th, three days from now. Brenda was furious.

"We won't have any buddy poppies!"

Each year, the ladies pinned green ribbons to poppy stems and sold them during the parade along Main Street. The flower commemorates fallen wartime comrades-in-arms, or buddies, thus the name. Proceeds supported veterans and their families.

"What do you mean?" Felice asked.

"Last month, I wrote a note for Charlene Holt to fax an order to Murphy's Nursery. As you know, they've been supplying our poppies for the past 10 years. They were to deliver 1000 blooms yesterday, May 21. When I called Robbie Murphy this morning to see why they hadn't arrived, he insisted the order was for 7000 blooms, for delivery on May 27.

"That's two days *after* the parade! What on earth was he thinking?"

"It's right here," Brenda said, waving a copy of the requisition with her note attached.

"What a mess! That nursery's been sliding downhill since Old Man Murphy retired and Robbie took over," Felice complained.

"He's been making weird mistakes lately. Did you hear about the white lilies Howard Butler's widow requested for his funeral? Robbie delivered them to the chapel the day of Maeve Hicks's wedding, instead of the pink peonies she ordered. She was red-faced—but not in a blushing bride way."

"It's because he can't stop thinking about Charlene."

After working three years in Montreal, Charlene had moved back to care for her ailing dad. She volunteered part time at the auxiliary.

"They're gaga over each other. She's just as bad. *Robbee* this, *Robbee* that," Brenda said, mimicking the French accent Charlene had picked up.

Just then, Hazel Peters, another volunteer and a high school teacher, walked in.

"What's wrong?" she asked, seeing their faces.

Hazel shook her head when they explained.

"I thought *I* had problems. Half my French class flunked their finals. That means I'll be teaching summer school again," she griped.

"I'll call Robbie to see if he can fix things," Felice said, seeing Brenda was still fuming.

"It's written right here in plain English, 1000, May 21," she repeated, slapping the papers on the desk.

Hazel picked them up and read the instructions.

When she broke out laughing uncontrollably, Brenda and Felice looked at each other, both at a loss.

Ω

What cracked Hazel up?

Solution: One of a Kind

Charlene had become accustomed to adding an angled line to the top of her numeral 1's, making Brenda's 1's look like 7's. This caused Robbie to misread the order. Hazel, a French teacher, immediately saw what had happened.

Salon Con

Hallie Brent was in tears as she and her best friend, Ava Robbins, sat on a park bench across the street from Ava's real estate office. Hallie had called her an hour ago after being fired.

"I've worked there for three years. I can't believe Margo thinks I'd steal," she said, wringing a crumpled tissue.

Hallie was a stylist at Margo's House of Beauty. Margo Flint, the salon owner, had accused her of taking $200 from the cash box under the front counter and fired her.

"I've known you since both of us were in pigtails and braces. You're no thief. Wasn't the box locked?"

"Not during business hours. We all had access to make change for cash customers."

"Three other people work there. Did she even consider that it could've been Emmy, Pam, or Jasmine?"

"Margo's had it in for me since I asked for a raise, which she refused."

"I'm one of her regulars, and she knows you're my friend. She also knows I'm on the village board, the zoning commission, play golf with the mayor's wife, and can make trouble for her. Let's march over there right now and get to the bottom of this."

"I'm too ashamed. We were in her office with the door open while she was yelling at me. Wanda Hayes was getting a perm and practically squirmed in her chair while I gathered my belongings. I thought she'd fly out the door with her hair half done. We both know why she's called The Mouthpiece."

Fifteen minutes later, Ava stormed into the salon. Emmy was finishing a haircut, and Pam was applying a color treatment. Jasmine sat at her manicure station doing her nails between customers. Ava headed straight for Margo, who was blow drying Darlene Houston's hair.

"What's this nonsense about Hallie stealing?"

"I don't have to explain personnel matters to you," Margo said with more bravado than she felt.

"Explain to me or to my husband who, as you know, is an attorney. He'll sue you for slander and damages for making unfounded allegations."

The color drained from Margo's face.

"Now tell me what happened."

"I always load the box with a stack of bills totaling $200. At 2:00, when I opened it to make change for a cash transaction, the stack looked suspiciously low, given that we'd been unusually busy."

"You close in two hours. Make sure no one leaves before I get back. I intend to have a chat with everybody," Ava said, not waiting for a reply.

At 5:30 sharp, she returned and found Margo in her office, nervously shuffling papers. She closed the door, ignoring the worried looks the others exchanged.

"Why didn't you call the police?"

"I didn't want the bad publicity. Plus, she asked for a raise, which I couldn't afford. She's the logical suspect."

"There's nothing logical about that. Send Emmy in and wait outside," she ordered.

"My clients used credit cards. I had no reason to go near that box," Emmy insisted.

"Nothing looked odd when I gave Vickie Hardin her change around noon, Pam said."

"I only had one manicure and one pedicure, both paid with credit cards. My station's near the front desk, so I would've noticed anything suspicious," Jasmine said.

Ava called the others back in, ignoring Margo's obvious resentment at being bossed around in her own shop.

"One of you is lying."

$$\Omega$$

Who does Ava suspect?

Solution: Salon Con

Margo took her own money. If she was worried about bad publicity, she wouldn't have left the door open while yelling at Hallie, knowing The Mouthpiece was within earshot. Had she given Hallie a raise, the others would've demanded one as well. Framing Hallie gave her an excuse to eliminate one payroll expense. None of the staff would've thought twice about Margo removing her own cash.

Game Plan

G us Wilton came downstairs for his morning coffee, which he always sipped from one of the #1 Dad mugs Ellis, his son, had given him over the years.

A note was next to the coffeemaker: "Happy Father's Day to a Grand Dad!"

Gus smiled. An only child, Ellis was 12 when his mother died, making father and son exceptionally close. They went on camping and fishing trips, built model airplanes, and flew kites when weather permitted. Until he left for college, Ellis helped out at Gus's hardware store.

Their only rough patch hit when Gus announced his intention to propose to Cassie Marks.

"I won't call her Mom," Ellis, then 17, protested.

"Son, no one can replace your mother. Just please give her a chance."

Ellis and Cassie forged a peaceful coexistence that eventually blossomed into a friendship.

Gus's wife came downstairs, interrupting his reverie.

"Twenty-four years old and still your baby boy," she teased, seeing the note.

"I wonder what's up his sleeve this year."

"You'll see."

"You know something?" he asked, seeing her mischievous smile.

She answered with a mouth-zipping gesture.

When Ellis was 15, he started turning Father's Day into a game by planting notes with clues about what the current year's gift might be. That first year, he left a note under the wiper blade of Gus's van: Dad's a good **S**port. **P**atient. **O**ptimistic. **R**eliable. **T**ender. The emphasized letters spelled out *SPORT*. The gift turned out to be a year's subscription to *Outdoor Warriors* magazine, which Ellis paid for by secretly doing odd jobs around town.

Another year's message, "Dad Has My Back," was prelude to a framed photo his mom had taken of him on his bike after his dad removed the training wheels. The photo was blurred because they were in motion, with Gus following behind—not too close but at the ready. Ellis made the frame himself.

The tradition continued after he left for college. Gus got a note or email, followed by a package or gift card.

After he married and was lucky enough to land a job near his hometown, Ellis and his wife, Brynne, bought a house 20 minutes away.

"Any luck?" Cassie asked later as they were leaving to meet the kids for the traditional Father's Day dinner.

"Zilch. Nada. I'm stumped."

"Better take this along," she said, grabbing the note.

Two hours later, the four were having dessert when Ellis nudged his dad and winked.

"So what do you think?"

"I give up."

"Read the note out loud," Brynne suggested, beaming.

"Happy Father's Day to a Grand Dad!"

"Hmm. Read it again, Dad."

What's going on here? Gus wondered but played along as three faces glowed like northern lights.

"Maybe this'll help," Brynne said, taking the note, pulling a pen from her purse, and scribbling something before giving it back.

$$\Omega$$

What had Gus missed?

Solution: Game Plan

The mark Brynne made closed the space between the words *Grand* and *Dad,* resulting in the word *GrandDad.* The note was her and Ellis's way of announcing this year's Father's Day gift—Gus's first grandchild—which would arrive six months later. Cassie, of course, was in on the scheme.

Not So Secret Journal

Maud Pugh and her next-door neighbor, Bea Atwater, were in Maud's kitchen enjoying coffee and Bea's fresh-baked banana nut bread, a neighborhood favorite.

"I should bake a welcome loaf for our new neighbors across the street," Bea said.

"I see they're still unloading boxes."

Their visit was interrupted by the sound of feet running down the front stairs, a door slamming, and the high-pitched voice of Crystal, Maud's 16-year-old daughter

"*MOMMMM!!!!*" she screamed, racing down the back stairway that led to the kitchen.

"Uh-uh. Another war of the siblings. That's my cue to evacuate. Call me when there's a cease-fire," Bea said on her way out.

"Where'd they go?" Crystal demanded, gathering her robe around her, wet hair streaming.

"Who?" Maud asked, following her outside

"Alright, who was it?" Crystal said through clenched teeth, glaring at her 18-year-old brother, Ryan, and a boy about the same age she'd never seen before. They were standing in the driveway, talking. At least that's what it looked like.

"What's going on?" Maud asked, looking from her daughter to the boys.

"While I was in the shower, someone sneaked into my room. I heard noises when I turned the water off. By the time I grabbed my robe and opened the door, he—or they— were running down the back stairs, and my journal was on the floor."

For her birthday last year, Crystal's parents gave her a passcode-protected journal, an update on the lock-and-key diaries she'd been keeping since she was 13. She wrote in it regularly, more often since becoming smitten with Jeffrey York. They started exchanging shy glances after being teamed up in junior-year biology lab.

Because this journal was digitally protected, Crystal thought it was safe to hide it in plain sight and therefore kept it on the top shelf of her cluttered bookcase. A recent entry recorded her latest secret: "I'm sure Jeffrey likes me, but I'll probably have to make the first move."

Unfortunately, Ryan was a senior at the same school and had learned of the flirtation and teased her nonstop. He and his posse had taken to calling Jeffrey York the Dork.

"He's like a lovesick puppy—a Yorkie!" he snorted, pleased with himself.

"What's all the yelling?" her 12-year-old brother, Joey, asked, coming from the garage.

As far as Crystal was concerned, Joey was her *real* brother. She told everyone the hospital had sent Ryan home with her parents because his real parents wouldn't claim him. *Could Joey have gone over to Ryan's dark side?* she speculated.

"Maybe all three of them are in on it," she told her mom.

"What do you boys know about this?" Maud asked in her Mom-means-business tone.

"I've been in the garage working on my bike for at least an hour," Joey said, looking hurt.

"I'd be in mortal danger if I went anywhere near The Queen's chamber," Ryan replied in mock terror.

"My sister would kill me if I touched her diary, even one requiring a password," the new boy said.

"And who're you?" Maud asked, sizing him up.

"I'm Luke. We just moved in across the street. Ryan invited me to shoot a few hoops," he said, backing away.

"Not so fast, buddy," Maud said, both hands on her hips.

Ω

Why does Maud suspect Luke?

Solution: Not So Secret Journal

Luke let it slip that he knew Crystal's journal required a password. After bringing him upstairs to see his video game collection, Ryan convinced him to take the journal after showing him where Crystal's room was. Ryan meant to hide it and watch his sister squirm. Eager to make a friend, Luke agreed. But once in her room, he panicked and dropped it before fleeing, making the noise she heard.

Cupid the Trickster

Sophia, Deanna, and Brittany, three sisters, had grown up with parents who turned holidays into grand occasions, complete with elaborate decorations, games, and theme foods. The upcoming Valentine's Day was no exception.

Their parents had moved to a warmer climate, but the adult sisters, who lived within 30 minutes of each other, continued the tradition.

Brittany and Jake were expecting their first child, Deanna had recently married Nicholas, and Sophia had been working at the library since graduating from college two years ago.

Deanna and Nicholas were hosting the holiday at their new home.

"I'll make my tomato pesto shrimp, and we'll have a game show with love-themed questions," she said as the three were having lunch together."

"I'll bake Mom's red velvet cake," Brittany offered.

"I'll bring Phillip," Sophia said, ignoring their snickers because cooking was not among her skills.

She and Phillip had been dating a little over a year.

"I think he's the one," she'd said a number of times.

When the big day came, the three couples moved to the living room after dessert.

"Game time!" Deanna announced, opening a cabinet and bringing out a basket containing gift-wrapped boxes.

"There are five boxes, one for each of you, tagged with your name—"

"—Don't you get one?" Sophia interrupted.

"Nope, because I'm the emcee and I know what's in them," she said.

"Can we open them now?" Jake asked.

"*Patience!* A question is folded inside each box. After you open yours, read the question aloud. The first with the answer must ring this bell," she said, jangling a silver bell on the coffee table. You'll open them in alphabetic order by name. You start, Brit.

The room was quiet except for the sound of paper ripping.

Brittany's box contained a lavender aromatherapy candle and the question "What song title means 'Give Me Gentle Affection'?"

Phillip grabbed the bell.

"Love Me Tender!"

Jake's box held a personalized money clip and the question "What movie title means 'Breezy Departure'?" He grabbed the bell, shouting "Gone with the Wind!"

Nicholas, an environmental activist, found reusable drinking straws in his box, with the question "What song title means 'Greetings'?"

Sophia rang the bell.

"'Hello'—I *love* Lionel Richie!"

Inside Phillip's box was a Swiss army knife with the question "Who are two famous star-crossed lovers?"

"Romeo and Juliet," Nicholas called, bell in hand.

Finally, it was Sophia's turn. Her box contained only a folded note. She thought her gift had been left out by mistake. When she unfolded the note and read it, she burst into tears.

Ω

What did Sophia find?

Solution: Cupid the Trickster

She found a note with the question "Will you marry me?" signed by Phillip. When a diamond ring with a ruby heart fell onto her lap, she shrieked. Everyone had known beforehand that the evening would end with teary congratulations. No one bothered to tell Sophia she'd forgotten to ring the bell before answering her question with a resounding *Yes!*

Mardi Gras Murder

O n Fat Tuesday, the day before Lent started, Sarah Hodges, second wife and widow of wealthy Peter Hodges, lay dead on her dining-room floor. She'd been battered with a fireplace poker. The blood-spattered weapon was beside her.

At 2:30 that afternoon, after returning from errands, the housekeeper, Mrs. Rafferty, discovered the crime and reported it.

Detective Aubrey Gaudet arrived to take her statement.

"She left at noon to pick up her King Cake from Steinman's Bakery for tonight's feast she was hosting."

In the small university town, Mardi Gras celebrations were relatively low key—no grand parades, floats, flamboyant costumes, or rowdy revelers.

"Was anyone else here today?" Gaudet inquired.

"At 1:00, I was leaving to run errands when Mr. Dawes, her lawyer, dropped by with papers for her to sign and left. When I returned, I found her like that."

Later that day, Gaudet sat across from Attorney Kenneth Dawes, a sharp dresser in his 40's. He wore a tailored three-piece suit and a silk tie Gaudet was sure hadn't come off a retail rack. The office was equally polished, white paneling and white leather upholstery.

"Did you speak with Mrs. Hodges today?"

"I went there with documents she'd requested, but she wasn't home. I phoned later only to hear the shocking news from Mrs. Rafferty," he said, wiping his face with a dingy handkerchief.

"Any idea who'd want to harm her?"

"I hate to say this, but there was bad blood from the outset between her and Peter's daughters. They resented his remarrying so soon after their mother's death and spoke ill of Sarah to anyone who'd listen. In retaliation, she convinced Peter to reduce their monthly stipends, forcing them to find part-time jobs."

By 5:30, Gaudet was back at headquarters interviewing the sisters.

"Sarah liked to torment us," Madeline declared.

"Explain," Gaudet prodded the 20-year-old wearing a waitress uniform.

"Before she invaded our lives like a virus, the three of us were continuing Mom's Mardi Gras tradition. After our Fat Tuesday dinner, she'd bring out a King Cake in which a tiny plastic good-luck charm was hidden. We'd each cut slices to see who got the good luck trinket."

"But Sarah ruined it," 22-year-old Stephanie said, her face contorted with fury. "After Dad's death, she replaced the inexpensive bauble with a piece of Mom's good jewelry, just for the fun of it, not caring about its value."

"Knowing we'd have to sell the jewelry to pay bills turned her on. She swore she'd find a way to cut off our allowance entirely," Madeline added, her voice shaking.

"Sometimes she'd show up at the shoe store where I work, have me bring out a dozen pairs of shoes without buying anything. She knew my pay's commission based," Stephanie said.

"Sounds like you all had motives, but I don't think either of you killed her."

Ω

What bothers Gaudet about this case?

Solution: Mardi Gras Murder

Dawes's immaculate attire and pristine office are inconsistent with the dingy handkerchief he used. Returning later that day and finding Sarah alone, he begged her again not to break up with him, and again she mocked him. He lost it and did her in with the first thing he saw, a poker. He dirtied his handkerchief wiping ash residue from the handle.

Tough Irish Luck

M ike O'Toole's pub, the Lucky Leprechaun, had been vandalized during the night.

"Bums kicked the door in. So much for Irish luck, eh?" Mike grumbled while Alex Jonas, his insurance agent, checked a window near the damaged back door.

It was 10:30AM, and Jonas had had only two hours' sleep, thanks to an inconsiderate newborn.

"You gotta see what they did inside," Mike said, pulling him around to the front door.

Tables and barstools were toppled, and some had broken legs. The place was coated with dried foam from Mike's best Irish stout. Fortunately, the mirror behind the bar remained intact.

"I closed at 1AM as usual. Returned at 9:00 and found this."

"It's a mess alright," Jonas said, making notes.

"I'll have to cancel the St. Pat's shindig. I already called Maggie."

For the past 15 years, the Lucky Leprechaun had treated customers to free beer and Maggie's famous Irish soda bread as part of the annual celebration.

"Who's got it in for you?"

"I fired Archie Hicks last week for playing video games on his phone during work hours. I'd warned him several times and finally had to let him go."

Jonas found Archie at his apartment.

"I wasn't happy about being fired, but I started a better job yesterday at the Boar's Head Taproom. The owners added an all-night video arcade. I work midnight to 8:30 maintaining the gaming machines."

The agent was heading to his office, trying to remember what a good night's sleep felt like, when he ran into Carol Mulligan, a sales rep at the radio station.

"Hey, Alex. How's the little guy? Never mind, I can tell from the way you look."

"Meredith and I have to keep reminding ourselves we were ready to start a family."

"Mike O'Toole called the station to make an annoucement. I hear somebody wrecked his place. More likely, he and Maggie had another of their famous brawls."

Carol could spread gossip faster than chocolate could melt in a sauna.

"Guess I'll talk to her," he sighed.

"Good luck. Maggie's the bear you poke at your own peril," she said laughing as she went on her way.

Maggie was on her front porch checking the mailbox.

"I just spoke with Mike and want to get your take on things while details are fresh in your heads."

"Speaking of heads, you'd better examine Mike's."

"Why's that?"

"Told the ol' fool a dozen times we need better security, especially for that rickety back door. Every time you pushed it open, those rusty hinges creaked like Dracula's casket in an old movie."

"That so?" Jonas said, more awake than he'd been all morning. "I'm going back to the pub. I overlooked something," he said, rushing out.

Ω

What did the sleep-deprived agent miss?

Solution: Tough Irish Luck

Jonas *heard* Mike say the door had been kicked *in* but never checked it himself. Maggie said the door opened by pushing it *out*. Competition from the Boar's Head Taproom was ruining Mike's business, and he couldn't afford another free beer bash. He vandalized his own place so he could file an insurance claim while still saving face in the community.

Garden Jargon

As if telemarketers and scammers weren't nuisances enough, the recent resurgence of door-to-door peddlers was becoming another infringement on Sadie Keen's peaceful retirement.

"I thought door-to-door sellers went the way of vacuum cleaner and encyclopedia pushers," she complained to Cynthia ("Cindy") Mack, her next-door neighbor. They were on Sadie's side porch sipping ice tea and enjoying their garden views.

"It's not like the good old days, when a salesperson was just that. Now you have to beware of shady characters face to face," Cindy said.

"The world's changing, and not for the better, I'm afraid."

Both women were widowed, lived alone, and had resided on the same block for more than 30 years. Sadie was president of her garden club, and Cindy volunteered as a baby cuddler in a hospital neonatal unit.

"At least I've got good old Rascal here to protect me," Sadie said, looking fondly at the 6-year-old Boxer lying in the corner. Rascal's ears perked up at hearing his name, but he lost interest when no treat was in sight.

"Your garden's at its peak—so many colors and textures. My Herb had the green thumb. Fortunately, Henry Stokes comes once a week to keep ours under control."

"I don't know how much longer I can maintain mine on my own. I might have to start borrowing Henry."

Just then, an unfamiliar white van came down Sadie's driveway. A sign on the side panel read "Ace Landscaping Experts," under which was a local phone number. A clean-cut man in his 30's, dressed in khakis, emerged and strode toward them flashing a 100-watt smile.

Rascal stood, ears and tail up.

"Good afternoon, ladies. I'm Jack Slye, owner of Ace Landscaping Experts, a new business on the other side of town. I'm driving around introducing myself and couldn't help but notice these two beautiful yards. Do you know if the owner's home next door?

When neither answered, Slye continued, keeping an eye on Rascal.

"I wanted to tell both residents about my introductory limited-time offer."

"I do my own gardening," Sadie said.

"Well, I'd be glad to walk around and offer suggestions. Even as we speak, I see an empty spot over there between the fence and the dog house. An azalea plant, or maybe some mums, would be perfect there."

"Tell you what, Mr. . . . . *Slye* is it? Sadie said with a poison-dart smile, "Get off my property immediately, or I'll call my son. That's who lives next door. He's a police officer, by the way."

As Slye backed his van down the driveway faster than he'd entered, Rascal gave a dismissive sniff and returned to his corner.

"What on earth, Sadie? Your Bobby teaches high school in another state. Why tell such a fib?"

"It's a good way to repel door-to-door vermin—and to out-con a con."

Ω

What two things made Sadie smell a rat?

Solution: Garden Jargon

No "expert" landscaper would refer to an azalea as a plant—it's a *shrub.* Azaleas and mums can be toxic to dogs, causing anything from digestive problems to inflammation, impaired heart rate, and death. Slye's offer to "walk around" was a pretense for scoping the place out.

Lethal Landscape

J ust as Sheriff Avery Watkins pulled into his parking spot, his phone rang. It was his dispatcher.

"Somebody bludgeoned Miles Hawthorne to death last night. His sister called 911."

Hawthorne had made his real estate fortune buying out families hit by hard times, forcing them to sell at considerable losses, with some filing for bankruptcy. He wouldn't be missed.

Approaching Hawthorne's unplowed driveway, the sheriff admired the landscape. It was covered by a blanket of pristine snow, thanks to last night's snowfall that added another 10 inches. It looked more like a holiday card winter wonderland than a murder location.

The coroner met him at the door.

"They really did a job on the poor guy. Body's in the library."

"Where's the sister?"

"Waiting in the parlor."

Miles's body lay on a blood-soaked Oriental carpet. An overturned desk chair, laptop, lamp, and other desk contents were nearby, all blood-spattered.

"Desk faces the patio, door's locked from inside," the sheriff observed.

"He was attacked from behind. Perp entered through the kitchen door."

"I'll check outside while you finish up here."

Other than a line of uneven footprints near the jimmied kitchen door, the snow was undisturbed.

Back inside, the sheriff sat facing Hawthorne's sister. Unmarried and only in her mid-30's, Gladys Hawthorne already had the lined features and pinched looks of someone much older.

"Miles was still in the dumps over his divorce, so often he'd call me over to fix dinner and stay the night. Last night after we finished eating and I cleaned up, he remembered paperwork he had to finish, so I went to bed."

"Doesn't look like the place was ransacked. Did you hear anything unusual?"

"After two glasses of wine, I'm out for the count."

"And this morning?"

"I came down to make coffee but saw the library lights still on. Miles sometimes sleeps—slept—in there. Then I saw him, like that," she said, looking away.

"You called 911 immediately?"

"Yes, my cell phone was in my pocket. I spoke loudly in case the killer was still in the house. I felt a draft from the kitchen, peeked inside, and saw the door cracked open. Footprints clearly indicated the killer had left."

"Who'd want him dead?"

"Who *didn't?* But talk to Maggie Pierce and Ed Riley."

"Why them?"

Miles was turning the Pierce homestead into a gaming casino, and he'd recently fired Ed, his accountant."

Sheriff Watkins waited outside the café where Maggie Pierce worked as a cashier. He recognized her from a distance, due to her stocky build and her limp.

"That's Karma for you," she said of Miles's fate.

"I understand you disapproved of his casino plans."

"My family owned that property for three generations. It broke my heart to sell it for peanuts, and now I'm working in a diner and facing financial ruin. But I wasn't the only one he exploited. Ask anybody."

Ed was in his office.

"Miles couldn't deal with his ex and me being romantically involved. Can't say I blame him, though. Nor would I kill him. I've been out of town on a two-day business trip. My flight landed this morning, and I can show you my boarding pass."

Later that afternoon, while transcribing the sheriff's notes into a formal report, Helen Fielding, his assistant, marched into his office, cranky as usual.

"How's a person supposed to read this chicken scratch?" she barked, showing him what she'd typed so far.

While correcting her mistakes, the sheriff came across something pointing to the identity of Miles's killer.

"Helen, you just saved me a lot of time."

Ω

Who does Sheriff Watkins suspect?

Solution: Lethal Landscape

Gladys described footprints "clearly indicating" the killer left, meaning prints going in one direction— away from the door. The sheriff's notes, however, mentioned "uneven footprints." Some impressions were superimposed due to the killer arriving and leaving, but several undisturbed prints showed one foot sinking deeper into the snow than the other. That would happen only in the case of someone who limped—someone like Maggie Pierce.

Secret Bunny

E sther, is anything wrong?" Mrs. Hardy, the head librarian, asked during a lull at the public library's front desk. Once again, she'd caught Esther Garcia gazing out the window while clients waited in line.

Esther was preoccupied with the curious events of the past six days. While leaving for work, she'd found a total, so far, of three Easter baskets left on her front porch overnight, the donor anonymous. Each basket contained a hand-printed note: "From a bunny 'hopping' to win you over."

The first basket contained a cellophane-wrapped lamb cake. The second one was filled with a dozen fresh-cut daffodils. Inside the third was a hollow chocolate bunny in a gold foil box.

"Obviously a secret admirer, and Easter's next week. It's a love story in the making," Mrs. Hardy, who loved romance novels, gushed after Esther explained.

"They must have been left after I went to bed. I wonder who it could be."

"Someone too shy to come forward," she said before her attention was required elsewhere.

As usual, Esther spent her lunch break at Bonner's Diner with her best friend, Winifred ("Winnie") Davenport, whom she'd told about the anonymous gifts.

"I bet it's Gerald," Winnie said, referring to the diner's owner.

"That's crazy. We've been friends for years. He and Carlos went to school together," she said, glancing at Gerald sitting at the register reading a book.

"Am I the only one who thinks you should have someone special in your life again?"

Three years ago, Esther's husband, Carlos, died from a sudden heart attack. Now most of her time was spent with work, volunteering, yoga, gardening, and her book club.

"Winnie, I'm still getting used to being a widow."

"Speaking of widows, maybe it's Everett Dyson. His wife died last year. As a pastry chef, he'd know his way around a lamb cake."

"But why Easter? Why now?"

"Spring fever? New beginnings?"

"The secrecy's so weird."

"What about that new guy across the street from you? You met him, right? He'd know you're in bed once your lights go off. *Eeeww,* a night-walking basket case!"

Esther had had no reason to mention that, as she headed out to work last week, her new neighbor, Farley Holmes, had introduced his partner, Devin Pierce. The two held hands and wore matching robes.

"Um, I doubt it's Farley. I'd better get back to work. I'll figure it out later.

"Okay, Ms. Sherlock, let me know when you crack the case."

Saturday morning, Esther and Everett ended up next to each other in the post office line.

"Do you know anything about Easter baskets left on my porch during the night?" she asked.

"I'd be your bunny if the job's open."

"That's not an answer."

"Isn't it?" he said with a flirty grin just as his turn came at the window.

"Solved the case yet?" Winnie asked on Monday.

Before she could answer, Gerald came with coffee refills. In one of those slow-motion action moments, Winnie was out the gate.

"Say, Gerald, Esther has a mystery bunny delivering gifts and sweet notes. You know anything about, say, a chocolate rabbit?"

"Well, whoever it is should've tucked a dinner invitation inside that rabbit," he said, blushing as he walked away.

"Winnie, I could kill you. But if I did, you wouldn't know I cracked the case."

Ω

Who's Esther's secret admirer?

Solution: Secret Bunny

Only Esther's secret admirer would know the chocolate rabbit was hollow, that a note could've been tucked inside. Because he and Carlos had been friends, Gerald feared expressing his feelings, not wanting to jeopardize his and Esther's friendship. Esther, thinking maybe Easter, after all, was a time for new beginnings, took it upon herself to invite him to dinner.

Loretta Martin

Mother's Day Charm

(A version of this story appeared in *Woman's World*.)

There's been a robbery at the agency!"
Helen Warren's voice cracked as she and Ben
Malone rushed into the sheriff's office, where
Marlie Pearson, dispatcher and word puzzle addict, was
engaged in her morning routine of solving the daily Jumble
while having her first caffeine fix.

Helen owned Warren Insurance Agency, located a block
away. Ben was her sales agent.

Before Marlie could respond, Sheriff Ash Quinlan
walked in. He could tell from their faces that his workday
had begun.

"What happened?" he asked.

"Someone's taken the Mother's Day bracelet Helen got
for her mom, and—"

"—Let her tell me, Ben."

"When I arrived to open up, the front door was ajar, but I
didn't see anyone. While I was debating whether to go
inside, Ben walked up.

"I came early to fix a broken light fixture," he added.

Between insurance sales calls, Ben earned extra money repairing small appliances in his workshop. Ironically, given his profession, he Jerry-rigged whatever he could get away with to avoid paying for his own repairs or paying service fees. And it was no secret that Alice, his wife, reheated two-day-old coffee. Their penny-pinching lifestyle had earned them the nicknames Mr. Skin and Mrs. Flint.

"Anything else missing?" the sheriff asked.

"No, even though $300 was in an unlocked petty cash box on my desk," Helen said.

"Describe the bracelet," Quinlan prompted.

"Five antique gold letters, different sizes and styles, spelling out Mom's name—Celia. They were attached to a 24-carat gold chain. Hanover Jewelers assembled it as a special order for Dad before he died last year. He'd wanted the letters made into a charm bracelet for their 40th wedding anniversary, which happens to fall on Mother's Day this year, a week from today. He'd collected the letters from their many travels."

"How beautiful! Everyone knew how close Celia and your dad were," Marlie said, choking up.

When did you last see it?" the sheriff asked.

"Yesterday afternoon, after I picked it up from Hanover's. I had it polished and brought it to the office to show it off. Pearl tried it on, and so did Alice when she came by to pick Ben up early."

"We were leaving town for Alice's 20th high school reunion and had last-minute errands to run," Ben explained.

"Incidentally, Alice didn't think Rudy's joke about splurging on airline tickets instead of hitchhiking was funny," Helen said. "Anyway, I put it in my desk drawer before locking up."

"Who has keys?" Quinlan asked.

"Just the four of us who work there: Pearl, my assistant; Rudy, our claims adjuster; Ben; and me."

"Celia would've been thrilled," Marlie said, returning to her puzzle.

"Then it was an inside job," the sheriff concluded.

"But why steal something personalized and therefore easily identifiable?" Helen wondered.

"That *is* pretty bold. Let's go to your office so I can have a look around," the sheriff said.

As they were leaving, Marlie stopped them.

"Wait! I think I know which piece of this puzzle's missing. And I don't mean my Jumble." she said, looking like she'd just won the lottery.

Ω

What did Marlie know?

Solution: Mother's Charm

A word puzzle junkie, Marlie realized that the names Celia and Alice are anagrams. Wanting to impress her high school friends with antique 24-carat bling, Ben's wife convinced him to "borrow" the bracelet, rearrange the letters, and then reassemble them in time for the bracelet to mysteriously reappear before Mother's Day.

Halloween Heist

(A version of this story appeared in *Woman's World*.)

A t 10:30AM, Sheriff Hillary Strong was silently cursing whoever invented paperwork when Pearl Gage rushed into her office.

"Someone stole my ugly sweater!"

"Your what?" the sheriff looked up, puzzled.

"My Halloween sweater. It's missing!"

Each year, the local knitting club, the Knit Wits, hosted a pre-Halloween potluck at the community center. The evening ended with an ugly sweater competition, with contestants modeling their creations. The winner was awarded a $300 gift card to the Yarn Barn.

"But who'd take it?" Sheriff Strong asked.

"I've won three years in a row. There are only four other contestants this year. That's four suspects."

The town rumor mill had it that club membership and contest entries had declined dramatically.

"These four," she said, pulling a wrinkled clipping from her bulging tote. The article, titled "Ugly Sweater

Competition at Halloween Potluck," showed pictures of the sweaters, along with contestant names and photos.

Tricia Murdock's entry was green, with black stripes and snaggle-toothed orange jack-o'-lanterns. Helen Weaver's contender was purple with a slick-haired, black-caped vampire with dripping fangs. Bobby Jean Anderson fashioned a vest with alternate rows of gray skull and crossbones and black-clad witches on a red background. Millicent Treadwell's creation was bright yellow with green scalloped sleeves and miniature candy-corn buttons.

Sheriff Strong recalled the article, thinking they all deserved to win.

"Is that's real candy?" she asked.

"It's craft clay and resin, painted in candy-corn colors."

"Where were the sweaters?"

"In the center's office. I dropped mine off yesterday morning at 11:00. This morning, I remembered a missing button and returned when the center opened at 10:00 to replace it, but it was gone."

"I'll get statements from the ladies."

"Start with Tricia. We knitted our entries in secret, but she's been hinting that the contest is fixed and giving me the fish eye at meetings. Regular membership dropped in large part because of growing tension in the group."

Three hours later, the four had been summoned to the sheriff's department. Helen, Bobby Jean, and Millicent were in the outer office, waiting their turn to follow Tricia.

"It's no secret Pearl and I butt heads. I'd be an obvious suspect and a fool to take it," Tricia snapped.

"I was visiting out-of-town friends. Anyway, I figured my vest stood a pretty good chance of breaking Pearl's winning streak," Bobby Jean said with bubbly optimism.

"Between 9PM and 5AM, I was in the ER. My four-year-old had stomach problems. I brought him with me today because I couldn't afford a last-minute sitter," Millicent, a single mom, said, trying to console the cranky toddler squirming on her knee.

"I was at brunch with my daughter's Girl Scout troop at Larson's Diner. We finished an hour ago, and I have our time-stamped receipt," Helen said.

Sheriff Strong dismissed all but one of them.

Ω

Who took Pearl's sweater?

Five-Minute Cosy Mini Mysteries (with Solutions)

Solution: Halloween Heist

Millicent, a single mom short on money, stole the sweater. While dropping hers off at lunchtime and finding the unlocked office empty, she took it, knowing it was the one to beat. Unfortunately, her toddler, thinking the colorful candy corn buttons were real, managed to break one off and swallow it while Millicent was on the phone, which led to a night spent in the ER—and to a scary lesson about fair play.

24-Carat Turkey Trot

At 8AM, Detectives Maggie Stone and Dave Winters sloshed across Willard High School's unpaved parking lot, which was soaked from the morning downpour. They made their way through bustling students to the gymnasium office, where a flustered Principal Easton waited.

A short man with a slapdash comb-over and an eye tic, he'd reported an antique pin stolen from the office safe.

"Was anything else taken?" Stone asked, peering into the open vault.

"Not that I can tell after checking drawers and cabinets."

"What happened?" Stone asked, opening her notebook.

"At 6:45, Brian Avery, our head coach, phoned me at home to report the pin missing."

"Describe it," Winters said.

"A 24-carat diamond-studded Tiffany pin, shaped like a cornucopia, with ruby and emerald fruits spilling out. Worth $10,000. Both the Tiffany name and serial number are stamped on it."

"Why was it here?" Detective Stone asked.

"Mrs. Constance Fitzpatrick had donated it in her husband's name—he died recently at age 85. There was quite the buzz over their May–December marriage, as I recall. Anyway, she took the pin from their bank vault because she intended to award it personally to whoever won the turkey trot—

"—*Turkey trot?*" Winters asked.

Recently transferred from out of state, Detective Winters wasn't up to speed on local customs.

"The pre-Thanksgiving foot race scheduled for the day after tomorrow. The extensive media coverage made her nervous about keeping the pin at home, so she brought it here yesterday for safekeeping."

"Who has access and knows the combination?" Detective Stone asked.

"The janitor has a key, but only Coach Avery and Cynthia Dixon, the girls coach, have a key and know the combination. And I do, of course." he added.

"Where's Coach Avery?" Winters asked.

"He should be waiting downstairs."

They found him in the equipment room. At 6 feet 6 and 230 pounds, Avery looked ready for a sports magazine photo shoot. His designer sweats and high-end running shoes were spotless. A phone in a leather holster on one arm and a fitness tracking device attached to the other arm completed the look

"Walk us through what happened," Detective Stone said.

"I got here at 6AM and ran my daily laps around the track before going inside. Thirty minutes into my routine, Connie—Mrs. Fitzpatrick— called me, apologizing for the early hour. She couldn't find appraisal documents and had forgotten to record the pin's serial number. She asked me to get it and call her back. When I opened the safe, the pin was gone. I called Principal Easton and waited down here."

"Did you go anywhere after speaking with him?" Stone asked.

"No. I've been in here checking inventory."

"So either you, Easton, or the girls coach removed it," Winters concluded.

"I certainly didn't," the principal said, his twitch going into overdrive.

"I suggest you talk to Coach Dixon. Her nasty divorce and custody battle are costing her a fortune," Coach Avery suggested.

"That won't be necessary, Coach. We'll explain down at the station. Let's go."

Ω

Why is Coach Avery being taken into custody?

Solution: 24-Carat Turkey Trot

Avery's photo-ready looks were not those of someone who'd run laps around a rain-soaked track. He removed the pin and tried to implicate Coach Dixon. He and Mrs. Fitzpatrick ("Connie," he let slip) were romantically involved, and he'd convinced her to file a false insurance claim. Now they both would look like turkeys.

Poetic Device

D ad got another rose, Aunt Jess!" 12-year-old Brent Marsdon shouted as he bolted out the door. He was late for soccer practice.

"Whoa, Scamp! No kiss for your favorite aunt?" Jessica Worth called.

She smiled at the air-kiss he blew over his shoulder and headed for the kitchen, where her brother, Andy, was at the table reading a note. A fresh red rose lay nearby—the third anonymous delivery to his mailbox in a month. Each rose had been pinned to an unsigned note written in ink on fine stationery in the same tilted, lightly smudged handwriting.

Jess read over his shoulder.

Roses are red, violets are blue.
Someone hopes to get to know you.

"Is that even *poetry?*" she scoffed, setting down the cookies she'd brought.

"Who do you think is sending these?" Andy asked.

The previous notes were taped to the refrigerator.

*A perfect rose, pure and white
For someone who's such a delight.*

and

*This rose, a mellow yellow
Is for a very special fellow.*

"These are really bad. My sources indicate three possibilities."

"Only three?"

"I think you meant to ask, *That many?*" she teased. "There's Sadie Perlman, the librarian, who manages to bring your name up at every book club discussion. Randye Coates, your mail carrier, told a coworker she'd die happy drowning in your dreamy blue eyes. Now *that's* a smitten kitten!

They both groaned."

"Meryl Dyer, Brent's dental hygienist, is always asking if you're seeing anyone."

"I don't know whether to be flattered, embarrassed, or scared."

Widowed for three years, at 36 Andy missed that special connection, but his focus was on his son. For now, Jess's family, his charity work, an occasional dinner date, and his contracting business kept him busy.

The doorbell rang, halting their conversation.

"I forgot that reporter was coming," he said.

"I didn't. You think these cookies are for *you?*"

Katlyn Purdue, *The Sentinel*'s new features reporter, had scheduled an interview for the paper's profile on local business owners and the charities they supported.

"Hi. My previous interview ended sooner than expected. Am I too early?"

"Not at all. My sister's joining us in the kitchen."

"I appreciate your taking time," she said, trailing him.

Following introductions, the three settled around the table, which Jessica had cleared.

"Coffee and fresh-baked cookies?" she offered.

"I never refuse sweets. Lovely kitchen, Mr. Marsdon," she remarked, looking around the sunny room."

"Thanks. Jess keeps the place suitable for human habitation. Call me Andy."

"Let's get started," she said, pulling out a notepad and arranging it at a comfortable angle.

An hour later, Katlyn had left for her next assignment.

"Why keep these notes?" Jess asked, adding the latest to the refrigerator door.

"Not everybody has three secret admirers, Sis."

He noticed how intently she was studying the notes.
"What is it?"

"Hm, I'm thinking my sources might be wrong, that there's a new angle here."

Ω

What has Jessica so intrigued?

Solution: Poetic Device

Katlyn was Andy's secret admirer. Slanted, or "tilted," cursive writing is a sign of left-handedness. Lefties hook and arch the hand in an effort to write "normally," that is, left to right. Smudging can result from dragging the hand across the writing surface when writing in ink. She had to "arrange" her notepad at a comfortable angle before taking notes.

The Missing Tiara

A t 7:30AM, Detective Jill Beard rang the Westons's doorbell, setting off a racket inside. *Rinngg! Hellooo! Rinngg!*

A disheveled Hillary Weston greeted her, shushing their African Grey parrot, aptly named Squawker.

"Quiet, Squawker!" she called, steering them to the kitchen, away from the cage area, which took up a third of the sunporch between the living room and the patio. The bird was quivering on one of two perches in its domed cage.

Quiet Squawker! Good bird!

The Westons had purchased him two years ago when he was six months old. Greys are fairly intelligent and, in addition to characteristic clicks and trills, Squawker could mimic certain human speech patterns. He even seemed to sense moods and interacted well socially. Toys and scheduled TV time provided a steady stream of stimulation between his sleep cycles.

Okay! Good bird! Bye-bye!

"Squawker's all revved up today."

"More than usual. He knows something's wrong. It's my tiara. It's missing, and tomorrow's the 4th of July."

76

Leonard, her husband, gave her the crown, as he called it, four years ago to celebrate the opening of her yarn shop, Knit Tricks. A jeweler and retired military veteran, he'd designed it himself using red rubies, white diamonds, and blue sapphires. Hillary wore the headpiece on patriotic holidays and other special occasions.

As Detective Beard started taking notes, Leonard entered the kitchen, still in pajamas.

"What's wrong?"

"My crown's gone."

"Gone where?"

"Well, Lenny, now if I knew *where,* it wouldn't be gone, would it?"

"What happened?" the detective asked.

"I removed it from the upstairs safe yesterday morning, put it in my carryall, and took it to my shop. The carryall was in the back office. I left early, taking it with me to my hair appointment at Marlene's. Anne, my assistant, was to close up for me."

"Why take it to the beauty shop?" Leonard asked.

"To make sure it fit over my updo," she said as though talking to a child.

"Then what?" Detective Beard said.

"I returned home around 7:30, exhausted. I laid my carryall on the entry bench and went straight upstairs to put on the special turban Marlene gave me to protect my hair. I didn't even stop to greet Squawker or to undress. I stretched out for a nap but slept through the night."

"Neither of you heard anything?"

"I wouldn't have heard anything through layers of terrycloth, and Lenny sleeps wearing headphones."

"When did you notice it was gone?"

"When I came down and went to feed Squawker. Both the patio and sunroom doors were open."

"So Marlene and Anne knew it was with you," Detective Beard concluded before leaving.

Later that day, she interviewed them.

"After finishing Mrs. Weston's hair, I closed up, had dinner with friends, and was home by 8:00," Marlene said, indignant at being considered a suspect.

Anne was still at home.

"I closed at 6:30, did some housekeeping, and drove to Mrs. Weston's to drop off the day's take. She doesn't like leaving money in the register, and there's no safe. I rang the bell around 8:15 but left when no one answered. There was only the sound of the TV.

Back in her office, the detective kept going over her notes. Something wasn't right. Suddenly, it hit her. She was pretty sure who'd be watching tomorrow's fireworks from a jail cell.

Ω

Who does Detective Beard suspect?

Solution: The Missing Tiara

Anne would've heard more than the TV had she rung the bell, which never failed to set Squawker off. She owed back taxes, and the IRS was threatening to levy her wages and seize assets. Seeing the TV light, she walked around to the patio and found both doors unlocked. She sneaked in and cooed at Stalker to keep him quiet, then took the tiara from the unguarded carryall, hoping to sell it to pay her taxes.

A Tall Tale

At 9AM, Sheriff Willa Simmons and her deputy, Hank Pugh, arrived at Heath Publications, owned by Roger Heath. His assistant, Adrian Barnes, had reported a fatal accident.

"It's Damon Palmer!" he exclaimed, leading them to a conference room, where Palmer lay about two feet away from a seven-foot-tall bookcase next to the door, his skull crushed. A bloody bronze bust was next to his body, and one of his legs was caught in the rung of his overturned chair.

Heath had converted the first floor of his Victorian home, with its high ceilings and original woodwork, into editorial and administrative offices. He kept the second and third floors as his private residence.

Each year, he hosted a Weekend Fiction Bootcamp for local aspiring authors, who stayed on site for marathon writing workshops Heath led. The goal was for them to complete a short story worthy of inclusion in Heath's annual New Voices anthology. Only one story would be chosen.

This year's contenders were Sherry Eames, a petite bank teller; Chet Brewer, a six-foot-eight basketball coach; and Damon Palmer, a retired professional jockey.

"What happened?" Simmons asked.

"I arrived at 7AM to set up for the last day, and there he was. He must've bumped the shelf while reaching for a book and tipped the bust over."

"Has anyone else been in here?" Simmons asked, scanning the library turned conference room.

Two similar shelves were cluttered with books, folders, and more heavy-looking carvings and artifacts. A laptop was at the edge of the conference table, its screen facing the door. A rolling ladder was in one corner.

"Only Mr. Heath after I ran upstairs shouting for him. Sherry and Chet heard the commotion and started to follow, but he ordered them to wait in the upstairs parlor."

"Looks like that empty space is where the bust was," Deputy Pugh said, pointing to the second shelf from the top.

The two officers followed Adrian upstairs, where Heath, Sherry, and Chet waited.

"This is horrible! Why didn't he use the ladder? That bust weighs over 70 pounds," Heath cried.

"Was he in the library late at night, or did he come down before 7:00?" Sheriff Simmons wondered aloud.

"He'd been stuck on an ending and might've been working into the night and fell asleep," Sherry offered

"On my way to bed last night after having a snack, I asked if he wanted anything, but he was hunched over his laptop, engrossed and completely oblivious," Chet added.

"Damon's work showed such promise. What a shame this grizzly accident ended it," Heath said."

"But *was* it an accident?" Simmons murmured.

Ω

Why does the sheriff suspect foul play?

Loretta Martin

Solution: A Tall Tale

No books were on the floor, refuting the argument that the victim might've been reaching for one. At six-foot-eight, Chet Brewer was the only one tall enough to reach the bust without needing a ladder. Driven by jealousy over Heath's constant praise of Damon's work and the certainty his story would be chosen, Chet sneaked up behind him unnoticed and bashed his head in.

Bungled Burglary

A nna Farber pulled into her Aunt Vivian's driveway, where she saw a police cruiser, lights flashing and bubble spinning. Last week, Vivian West suffered a fall that resulted in a badly sprained ankle. Her doctor had instructed her to avoid putting weight on it, but knowing her aunt, Anna thought she might've disobeyed, making a bad situation worse.

"Aunt Viv, are you okay?" she called from the foyer.

"It's about time! I left a voicemail over an hour ago," Vivian complained from the library, where she reclined on a sofa, an ice pack against her jaw.

"I didn't see your call right away. Paul and I were at the movies with my ringer off. Your message said only that you needed help," Anna replied, letting the rebuff slide.

The library was in shambles. A porcelain table lamp was shattered, contents spilled from an end table drawer, and books from the bottom shelf of a bookcase were strewn across the floor.

"I could've been killed!" Vivian huffed.

Anna looked with wide-eyed alarm from her aunt to two uniformed officers.

"I'm Officer Beatrice Daley, and this is Officer Elias Hodgkins. Your aunt reported a robbery, and we're taking her statement."

"Any idea who it might've been, Mrs. West?" Hodgkins asked.

"*Ms.*" she snapped. "It's no secret I live alone and keep emergency cash around."

"I offered to find you a caretaker until Mrs. Truman gets back," Anna said.

"You're my only family. I'd hoped *you'd* be around, but apparently your new boyfriend—your *unemployed* new boyfriend—takes precedence," she shot back.

"What was taken?" Daley asked, noting the tension between them.

"The $900 I kept in there," she said, motioning to the open end-table drawer next to the sofa. "I scared them off before they could grab my Fabergé eggs and Chinese jade vases," she continued, gesturing at the top shelves of two tall lighted display cases.

"Not to mention your silver candlesticks," Anna added, pointing to the fireplace mantel.

"Luckily, they never made it to any other rooms," Vivian said.

The front and back doors are undamaged. Who else has keys?" Hodgkins asked.

"Edwin Pugh, my driver, and Mavis Truman, my housekeeper who's out of town on a family emergency. And you, of course," she added, scowling at Anna.

"I had nothing to do with this! What about Floyd? You haven't changed locks since the divorce, and he's in debt up to his ears."

"Thank goodness I made him sign a pre-nup. I hear he filed for bankruptcy," she said with smug satisfaction.

"Earlier, you said 'them.' There were more than one?" Officer Daley asked.

"I'm using my housekeeper's bedroom down the hall to avoid the stairs. I was getting ready for bed when I heard noises in here and immediately dialed 911. I crept toward the sound—obviously without thinking. As I got closer in the dim light, I heard two voices but couldn't make out words. A floorboard must've creaked as I moved, because two men ran out. One dashed out the front door, and the other smacked me before following his partner."

"That's awful! I'm so sorry I wasn't here for you," Anna said, close to tears.

"Did you recognize them?" Officer Daley asked.

"There wasn't enough light."

"What happened next?" Hodgkins prompted.

"I turned up the lights, limped to the kitchen for an ice pack, and waited for help to arrive."

"We'll need to interview the driver and the ex," Hodgkins said to his partner.

"Maybe, but first let's go over your story again, Mrs.— *Ms.*—West. Something doesn't add up."

Ω

What's bothering Officer Daley?

Loretta Martin

Solution: Bungled Burglary

The first thing a victim would've done would be to lock the door after assailants left. Even in dim light, burglars would've seen valuables in lighted display cases and the glint of silver candlesticks—but not cash in a closed drawer. Embittered by a third failed marriage and feeling abandoned, Vivian faked a robbery to draw attention. She didn't disturb collectibles on higher shelves because she couldn't bear weight on her sprained ankle. Nor would she have damaged such expensive items. As for the "missing" $900, it's under her sofa cushion. Facing a charge of filing a false police report, she tearfully apologized and retracted her statement.

The Vanishing Vase

At 9PM, a distraught Barry Lattimer, owner of Lattimer's Auto Towing and Repair, phoned his younger sister, Nicole.

"Someone stole Marge's vase!"

"What?"

"Her she shed gift is missing."

"Call Sheriff Holcum, I'm on the way."

For their upcoming wedding anniversary, Barry had converted a storage shed at the back of their property into a retreat for his wife, Marge, a photographer. Jason Crane, local handyman, helped install a flagstone floor and painted the structure in Marge's favorite color, cobalt blue. Parker Sanderson, an electrician, was upgrading the wiring.

"My own she shed! I can't wait to start decorating it," Marge gushed.

During her daily jog through town, Nicole had spotted a cobalt blue vase in the window of Stephan's Unique Antiques and texted Barry, attaching a photo and suggesting he also give Marge something to unwrap.

Hours were by appointment, so Nicole contacted the owner and invited herself along the following day.

"*Ja,* iss French crystal, mid-19th Century," Stephan Klein said in a thick German accent.

"It's fate! Crystal or glass is the traditional three-year anniversary gift," Nicole said as they left.

"I'm surprised at the low price."

"I hear the shop's tanking, forcing Stephan to sell his inventory on line."

The day before their anniversary, Marge was called out of town for a four-day photo shoot.

"We'll have a belated celebration at home," she'd said, trying to sound cheerful.

The doorbell interrupted Barry's reverie. Sheriff Holcum and Nicole had arrived at the same time.

"This was some kind of vase?" Holcum asked

Nicole showed him the photo on her phone.

"Stephan invited us to wait while he googled additional information, but we didn't have time. So, he offered to deliver the vase and printouts around 3:30 this afternoon," Barry said.

"Where was it?"

"We brought it to my office to unpack, but I had to leave—hydraulic lift malfunction at the shop. I returned around 7:00, fell asleep upstairs. When I woke, I came down to hide the vase, only to find it gone."

"Nothing else taken?"

"That's the strange part. Everything else appears in order. It didn't help that I left the patio door unlocked," Barry admitted, blushing.

"What about Jason and Parker?" Nicole asked.

"They knew we hung a spare back-door key in the garage in case we weren't at home."

"I'll look into it tomorrow," Holcum said, glancing at his watch.

The next day, he started with Stephan.

"Herr Lattimer's beeper sounds shortly after I arrive. He goes to patio outside office, closes door to make call. A few minutes later, he rushes back, says he must leaf at *vonce*. Vase iss on desk ven ve leaf together."

Parker was in his workshop.

"I saw it as I passed on my way to the basement to check the junction box. I'm single and live in a cabin. What do I want with some fancy-schmancy flower pot?"

Holcum summoned Jason to his office.

"My business is tools, not knickknacks," he snapped.

Three suspects, one of them a liar, Holcum was thinking later at dinner with his wife. Then it hit him. He knew who the culprit was.

Ω

Who vamoosed with the vase?

Solution: The Vanishing Vase

Upon researching the vase further, Stephan learned its value was three times what he'd sold it for, but he couldn't afford to make an offer to buy it back. He'd noticed that, in his haste to leave, Barry left the patio door open. Facing bankruptcy, he returned and pilfered it while Barry slept upstairs, hoping to auction it on line at a higher price.

The Last Word

(A version of this story appeared in *Short Fiction Break*.)

T*chlik-tchlik-thwomp-snik-snik!*
The noise shook Courtney Ferguson from a restless sleep. Before her senses adjusted to their unfamiliar surroundings, the sound stopped. She raced down the hall to wake her husband.

"It's 3AM, Courtney. What's wrong?" Jack asked.

"There's something's in the room. Or someone."

Another anxiety attack, he figured.

"We're alone in the house, and the alarm's on, Honey."

"*Something's not right in there!*"

Knowing better than to argue, he followed his wife down the hall, switching on lights. He listened from her bedroom doorway, hearing only the hum of the air conditioner hum. He went in, turned lights on, and checked the closet and adjoining bathroom. Nothing.

"Being back home, especially in this bedroom, is taking its toll. We should've booked a hotel room, he said."

"This is closer to the hospice."

91

Courtney, age 32, had returned to her childhood home, something she'd sworn never to do. Most of the house had been stripped to be put on the market, with only two bedrooms still livable. Courtney took her mom's room, but because it reeked of the heavy perfume she preferred, Jack's allergies forced him to sleep in the guest room.

"It's not my imagination. I heard a clattering, raspy sound, like dry gravel in a tin can."

"You're emotionally raw. You and your mother have been estranged for 10 years. The only reason you're back is because she's dying."

"And the only reason I know that is because she finally allowed someone to contact me."

Courtney would never forget how her mother—Mavis Dawson, former beauty queen—constantly berated her for perceived infractions.

"Stand up *straight,* Courtney! Do something about that hair! How *hard* can it be to lose a few pounds? Why're you home on a Friday night?"

Mavis's criticism was relentless, and Courtney's attempts to defend herself always ended with her mother having the last word. She was like a bush warrior celebrating victory by eating her opponent's heart. Mavis had navigated life, and her three marriages, using her looks, razor-sharp tongue, and obsession with having the last say on everything. As implausible it was, Courtney used to think her dad, Mavis's first husband, conjured his fatal aneurysm to escape her.

What did I do other than be born? she often wondered.

"Babe," Jack said gently, "despite her, you became the beautiful, compassionate woman I love."

"Dad would've loved you, as do I," she said, caressing his fuzzy cheek.

"We can still get a hotel room, you know," he said, pulling her into the hallway away from the odor.

"The doctors say it's only a matter of days."

Cancer had chewed its way through what had been Mavis's perfect size 8 body, eventually—and ironically—reaching her mouth. During their reunion, she went on auto-pilot, attacking her daughter and having the last word.

"I see you nevf learn nuffin' 'bout cosmethics."

Mavis's dentures no longer fit due to the lesions on her tongue, which distorted her speech.

"It's no surprise, Jack, that our last days together are spent in the same emotional freeze zone we've always inhabited."

Just as Jack braced for another sneeze attack, they heard a sound.

Tchlik-tchlik-thwomp-snik-snik!

It came from under the bed.

She felt Jack tense, which meant he heard it too.

Courtney watched her husband, ignoring dust bunnies and other lurking allergens, squat and peer under the bed.

She watched in horror as Jack fell into a sudden spasm of uncontrollable sneezing mixed with hysterical laughter.

Ω

What sent Jack into a fit?

Loretta Martin

Solution: The Last Word

Even on her death bed, Mavis had the last word. A spare set of her porcelain dentures with metal framework was trapped between a bed post and the iron grate of the air vent. They lay in the semi-darkness like two rows of translucent pearls. Each surge of the air conditioner set off a vibration—a "clattering, raspy sound, like dry gravel in a tin can."

Labor Day Meltdown

A t 7:30AM, Sheriff Helen Beaumont's radio woke her up with the weather report.

"Another 95-degree day, folks. Looks like Labor Day's gonna have 4th of July temps," the announcer said.

Any hopes for an easy day sank when her beeper went off on her night table.

"Somebody broke into Crystal Garrett's truck. She's got a freezer full of ice cream soup," the dispatcher said.

Crystal's brother-in-law, Frank Wharton, owned Frank's Vintage Auto Works and had retrofitted a Ford E450 step van for her dream venture of operating an ice cream truck. He cut an opening for a concessions window, upgraded the sound system, and installed a freezer lined with zinc cold plates for a refrigerant to keep contents frozen for up to 10 hours.

A local TV station had featured Crystal's new enterprise, Ice Cream Dreams on Wheels, announcing tomorrow's Labor Day grand opening. From noon to 7PM, the truck would be parked adjacent to the town square on Main Street.

A half hour after the dispatcher's call, Sheriff Beaumont pulled into Crystal's driveway and found her inside the truck in tears. Thick rainbow swirls of more than 15 flavors had puddled in the freezer.

"What happened?" Beaumont asked.

"Yesterday evening, the delivery team transferred my products to the freezer, which I'd pre-frozen. They unloaded dry goods and left by 6:00. I organized the supplies, rechecked the generator, and locked up. I set my alarm for 7AM and was in bed by 8:30. At 7:15, I went to check the truck and found the back doors pried open. The refrigerant should've kept my products frozen a while longer, but with the heat and open doors, everything melted faster."

"But the generator's still running," the sheriff said.

"Look at this."

There was an 18-inch space behind the freezer. Coil tubing connecting it to the generator had been pinched together, obstructing the refrigerant's flow and accelerating the ruin.

You heard nothing unusual?"

"I was zonked out, and the truck doesn't have an alarm."

"Any guess who's responsible?"

"*Three* guesses. Pete Lamont complained about my truck being parked near Chez Pierre, his hoity-toity bistro. Frank now wants to be paid, although he originally said he didn't because I'm family. I threatened to tell my sister. Greg Dyson's been spreading rumors that the work Frank did on the truck is substandard, although it passed inspection. He's mad because I rejected his inappropriate advances."

"Stay put 'til I talk to them."

At 10:00, Sheriff Beaumont rapped at the window of Chez Pierre, where Lamont was preparing for the 11:00 opening.

"My clientele shouldn't have to put up with that eyesore and its tacky music, but I wouldn't dirty my hands on it," Lamont sniffed.

After lunch, the sheriff knocked on Greg Dyson's door.

"I'll get him. He should be at work, but he's sleeping in," she said, her words dripping with sarcasm.

"My union was negotiating our contract between 9:30 and 12:30AM. Some of us then went to Wally's Pub, stayed until it closed at 3AM. Wifey here's still mad," he said, shooting her a sheepish grin she refused to return.

Frank was at his shop.

"Family's one thing, but I spent months and more than $4000 in materials modifying that rig. Why would I ruin it? Not to mention her sister would divorce me if I did anything like that."

By 3:00, Beaumont had interviewed the three suspects. After reviewing her notes, she made a beeline for the perp who'd spoiled Crystal's Labor Day labor of love.

Ω

Who's the culprit?

Solution: Labor Day Meltdown

Greg Dyson's the saboteur. A diehard union man, he was furious that Frank, having no union affiliation, had completed all that labor instead of hiring union workers. Plus, he was still chafing at Crystal's rebuff. On the way to his meeting, on an impulse he took a pipe wrench from his truck bed, jimmied the van doors open, and quietly took his revenge.

Music Box Blunder

"M arty, you got all dressed up for *me?*"
Detective Hannah Kincaid teased her partner,
Detective Martin Lowell, as he approached.
She'd been waiting for him outside the home of August
Quinn, eccentric billionaire philanthropist.

"Save it, Kincaid. This rental tux is on the clock, and
your page ruined my date night."

"It's 10:30. Is your date on the clock too?" she crooned.

"Very funny. What's up?"

"There's been a theft at August Quinn's home."

"You mean that rich . . . whatchamahoozie . . . germ nut,
right?"

"*Germophobe.* You're *sure* you passed the literacy test?"
she said, pressing the buzzer.

Dr. Weston Brooks admitted them.

"I'm Mr. Quinn's physician. Please remove your shoes
and wear these gloves. He has health concerns, which is
why he called me."

Lowell made "loose-screw" gestures as they followed
him to the living room, where Quinn lay on a sofa. Like all
seating in the room, it was covered in clear plastic.

99

"A music box was stolen? Where was it?" Kincaid asked, scanning the room, where nothing was out of order, not even an open magazine. Books were lined on shelves with military precision.

"Not just *a* music box but 19th-Century Swiss, hand-crafted, the size of a shoebox, burl marquetry, valued at $20,000. It was in there," he said, waving a gloved hand at a lighted case."

"What's marquetry?" Lowell asked.

"The wood inlay pattern," Quinn said with exaggerated patience

"Who was here today?

"Chef Maurice, Lara Cummins—she's my assistant—and the cleaners."

"Cleaners? You mean your servants?" Kincaid asked.

"Mr. Quinn employs a sanitation crew that comes twice a week," Dr. Brooks explained.

"What else?" she prompted, hoping no one else saw her partner roll his eyes.

"Lara dropped off paperwork this morning, the cleaners left at 4:30, and Maurice served dinner at 5:00, probably left an hour later."

"Probably?" Lowell said.

"I assume he saw himself out at 6:00, his usual time. I'd already gone upstairs. I was donating the box to charity, and before the messenger service collected it tomorrow morning, I wanted to review the paperwork. It was there when I came down at 6:30 to double-check the serial number. Back upstairs, I completed the documents, turned the stereo on, and dozed off while reading."

"When did you miss it?" Kincaid asked.

"At 9:00, when I came down for my nightly glass of milk and saw the open case."

"No signs of forced entry. Who has keys?" Lowell asked.

"Maurice, Lara, and Wes—Dr. Brooks."

"For emergencies," Brooks interjected.

"Give us their information, we'll interview them tomorrow," Kincaid said, ending the visit.

"Ever see a place so sterile place outside a hospital? He never invited us to sit down, even though everything's virtually laminated. The man's a robot," Lowell griped.

The following morning, they rang Maurice's bell.

"I left promptly at 6PM, in time to get to my part-time job as a sous chef. Mr. Quinn is quite tight-fisted. Whenever I brought up the subject of a raise, he'd swear he's on the brink of poverty."

Later that day, at Lara's apartment, while trying to control a rambunctious terrier, she explained her whereabouts.

"I was with friends until 8:00, came home, walked Rusty from 8:30 to 9:30. Is Mr. Quinn okay? He'd freak out being anywhere *near* a hospital."

"How'd you get the bruises?" Kincaid asked, ignoring her question after spotting purple blotches on both arms.

"Oh those," she blushed. "It's embarrassing. Yesterday morning at Mr. Quinn's, Rusty broke free and I fell chasing him down the newly polished hallway."

The detectives looked at each other, then at Lara.

"Rusty will need a new home, I'm afraid," Detective Kincaid said before slapping the cuffs on and reading her rights.

Ω

What gave Lara away?

Solution: Music Box Blunder

Knowing Quinn's fear of germs and his obsession with routine and order, Lara never would've taken Rusty to his home. She knew he'd be upstairs with his stereo going between 7:00 and 9:00 and then come down for milk. Her gambling habit had gotten her in deep water with the "friends" responsible for her bruises. She'd learned from the paperwork she delivered how much the music box was worth. She let herself in and took it, hoping to sell or exchange it to clear her debt. The box was found later in her bedroom closet.

About the Author

A s vice-president of my 8th-grade class, I thought I could do a better job than our president, so I composed an argument for his impeachment. Long story short: He was voted out, and I became president.

That's when I understood something I'd suspected since I was ten and making up stories and story snippets I kept in secret notebooks. Writing (and later editing) would play a huge role in my life. Over the years, that has turned out to be the case.

In July 2018, I added a new activity to my list of micro escapes from "real" writing and editing projects: reading short cozy mysteries—the shorter the better. It's fun trying to guess "who did it" before the scoundrel (and/or motive) is revealed.

I thought it might be an interesting change of pace to write this type of flash fiction. These 26 "cases" are the result of that effort.